PUFFIN

LATE K...

Margaret Joy was born on Tyneside, and has lived in
Bristol, on Teesside, and in other parts of the British Isles.
She started writing children's stories for radio and television when her own children were young. After teaching
for some years, she continued writing and has published
twenty books. She and her husband are now settled in
North Wales, where she enjoys living and writing in
beautiful surroundings.

Late Kick-Off

Margaret Joy

Illustrated by
Thelma Lambert

PUFFIN BOOKS

To David

PUFFIN BOOKS

Published by the Penguin Group
Penguin Books Ltd, 27 Wrights Lane, London w8 5tz, England
Penguin Books USA Inc., 375 Hudson Street, New York, New York 10014, USA
Penguin Books Australia Ltd, Ringwood, Victoria, Australia
Penguin Books Canada Ltd, 10 Alcorn Avenue, Toronto, Ontario, Canada m4v 3b2
Penguin Books (NZ) Ltd, 182–190 Wairau Road, Auckland 10, New Zealand

Penguin Books Ltd, Registered Offices: Harmondsworth, Middlesex, England

First published by Faber and Faber Limited 1990
Published in Puffin Books 1993
3 5 7 9 10 8 6 4

Text copyright © Margaret Joy, 1990
Illustrations copyright © Thelma Lambert, 1990
All rights reserved

The moral right of the author has been asserted

Printed in England by Clays Ltd, St Ives plc

Contents

Messages from the Match

Mr Bennet had flu. It began on Monday
when he woke up with a sore throat. On
Tuesday his eyes kept watering and he
couldn't stop sneezing. On Wednesday he
had a dreadful cold and his head was
throbbing. On Thursday and Friday, he
felt so bad that he just wanted to spend the
rest of his life in a warm place with his
eyes shut. – But the worst was over; by
Saturday he managed to get downstairs
and sit weakly in a chair by the fire.

'It's no joke being ill when you live all by
yourself,' he thought, and blew his nose
again. The television was on, but he shut
his eyes, so that he could just hear the
sound – the moving pictures and flashing
lights made his eyes water. A key turned

in the lock of the front door. His neighbour, Mrs Mannion, bustled in. She was carrying a tray on which was a covered plate.

'I thought you might be on the mend when I looked in yesterday evening,' she said. 'Now I've brought you a nice hot pie and some veg, and I hope you'll try to eat it.'

She helped to tuck a napkin under his chin, and placed the tray across his lap.

'I've still got a sore throat,' he grumbled.

'Well, eat what you can,' said Mrs Mannion soothingly, 'and I'll bring you some ice-cream later; that'll just slide down.'

Mr Bennet muttered and snuffled, but when Mrs Mannion had gone, he managed to eat most of the pie and all the carrots and beans. She came back ten minutes later, carrying a dish of raspberry ice-cream decorated with a wafer. She thought it looked very tempting, but Mr Bennet didn't say anything. He just took it from her and poked at the wafer with his spoon.

'What's this fancy thing?' he grunted.

'It's a wafer,' said Mrs Mannion. 'It's shaped like a fan, isn't it attractive? I saw a box of them in the supermarket and thought our Robbie might like to try them – and you too, of course,' she added.

'Huh-mmmf,' said the old man with a scowl – but he took a mouthful of the ice-cream and began to eat.

Mrs Mannion bustled round. She stood a flask of hot tea on the table next to him; she smoothed a thick rug over his legs; she put his tin of cough pastilles handy; she made sure the gas fire was just as he liked it.

'Well,' she said, glancing round with the empty dish in her hand, 'would you like a little snooze now? Shall I switch the television off before I go?'

'Certainly not, woman,' he snapped. 'What do you think I've got it on for? – City are playing at home this afternoon.'

'I know, I know,' said Mrs Mannion. 'Our Robbie's going to the match with Steve.'

'First time I've missed one of City's home games for five years,' grumbled Mr Bennet.

'I know, I know,' Mrs Mannion said again. 'The boys are really sorry you're not going with them as usual, but at least you can stay in the warm and watch it on the box, can't you?'

'It's not the same,' grumbled the old man. He scowled at the television set and added, '*And* it's my birthday – not that anyone cares . . .'

'Oh!' said Mrs Mannion. 'Why didn't you tell me, you – ?' (She nearly said, 'You silly, obstinate, old man,' but she stopped herself in time.) She went on, 'Robbie said I had to tell you they would be standing in the usual place by the half-way line right at the front. He said you were to look out specially, because you might see them on the television.'

'Huh,' said Mr Bennet, 'I'll see; I might . . . Now make sure you shut the door on your way out, woman – I don't want to be caught in a draught the whole afternoon.'

Mrs Mannion went out shaking her head over Mr Bennet. But she was used to him, and carefully closed the door behind her.

'He's just disappointed, poor old thing, that's what it is,' she said to herself.

When she got home, she told Robbie and his friend Steve about poor Mr Bennet.

'Poor old Bennie,' they said, 'Fancy missing the match on his birthday. – We'll bring him back a programme, that'll cheer him up.'

'And make sure you stand exactly where you always do,' said Robbie's mum, 'because he'll be looking out for you all through the broadcast.'

'Yes, yes,' said Robbie. 'If the cameras come our way, we'll make sure he sees us.'

Mrs Mannion went into the kitchen to make a cake; she had already decided that it was to be a birthday cake. Half an hour later the two boys came down the stairs.

They were laughing about some private joke. They already had their duffle-coats on, and now they swung their blue-and-white City-supporters' scarves round their necks.

'Just you keep out of trouble,' said Mrs Mannion.

'Don't worry about us,' said Robbie. 'We'll be in the family stand. – But keep an eye on the telly, Mum, you never know, you might see us.'

'Well, if I go to keep Mr Bennet company,' she said, 'I'll be able to watch it with him.'

The boys went off still chuckling to themselves at their secret joke. They reached the City ground, paid and pushed through the turnstile. They hurried along an echoing passage which opened out half-way up the terraces. Then they clattered down concrete steps to the lowest part of the ground. They pushed and zig-zagged through the crowd until they were down at the very front of the terraces near the players' entrance. Only a low wall stood between the crowd and the pitch. This was where they usually stood with Mr Bennet.

'This is the best place in the ground,' he always said. 'When you stand as close to the players as this, you can hear them swear, smell the turf, and see every move of the game.'

The boys leant on the dividing wall and looked round.

'Where are the TV cameras?' asked Steve.

'Over there, above the Press Box,' said Robbie, pointing to the platform at roof level opposite.

A camera man, wearing earphones, was already in place, turning a large camera on a stand, checking that everything was working before the kick-off.

'Do you think he'll focus the camera on us?' asked Steve anxiously.

''Course he will – whenever the play comes our way,' said Robbie, 'and especially if there's a throw-on from the line in front of us. – Have you still got your papers safe?'

'Yes, they're rolled up inside my duffle.'

'So are mine,' said Robbie. 'Old Bennie's going to get such a surprise. – Oh, look out, here they come.'

There was a sudden cheer mixed with a few boos. On came the visiting team, the Daffs, all in yellow, followed by City in their usual blue and white. They were greeted by much louder cheers from the home supporters.

'Quick now,' said Steve, 'let's do the first one while they shake hands and toss for it.'

Robbie put his hand in the top left side of his duffle-coat and pulled out a roll of computer paper. They unrolled it quickly, then leaned over and spread it flat along the front of the dividing wall, so that it could be seen only from the pitch – and by the cameras. They each held their hands over the top edge of the paper, so that it was kept in position.

Play began. The Daffs were determined

to win at all costs, so the game was rough
from the very start. After about five
minutes of play, the ball came thundering
across the pitch towards the boys.

'Now he'll see it!' exclaimed Robbie.

'Hope he's watching,' said Steve.

They needn't have worried. Old Bennie
was sitting forward in his armchair, never
taking his eyes from the screen; the moving
pictures and flashing lights didn't seem to

be affecting his eyes any more.

'Come on, City, you know what you've got to do,' he yelled. 'Thrash the blighters – Look at that! – You cheating, yellow-livered sw-sw-swine . . .' he spluttered, then stopped to cough. He opened his tin of cough pastilles. Then he paused to watch the ball thunder across the pitch to where he usually stood with the two boys. He froze with a pastille half-way to his mouth.

There on the screen *were* the two boys – he'd recognize them even at that distance in those duffle-coats – but what was that paper on the wall in front of them? It wasn't one of the usual adverts for banks or beer or building societies. Mr Bennet leaned even further forward and peered at the black lettering . . .

'HI, BENNIE' he read out loud. 'Hi, Bennie? – *I*'m Bennie – is that meant to be a message for me? It must be . . . cheeky young devils . . .'

He looked at the pastille he was holding

in mid-air and absentmindedly put it back
in the tin. His gaze returned to the screen.
At that moment, Tolly Robinson, the City
captain, neatly side-stepped his opponent
and jerked the ball up the field. The
crowd's roar grew louder. Mr Bennet
hammered on the arm of his chair.

'Come on, Tolly – shoot!' he yelled.

Tolly seemed to have heard him. He saw
an opening in the opposing defence and
shot. The ball curled through the air and
punched the back of the net. The two boys
leaped in the air and danced round one
another.

'First goal to us!' shouted Steve. Then he
added, 'Quick – where's the next
message?'

Robbie pulled a second roll of paper
from inside his coat. They flattened it and
draped it over the wall on top of the first
paper. As the players went back to their
positions, the cameras caught the boys'
length of wall again. It looked different.
Mr Bennet screwed up his eyes to look at it.

'A GREAT GOAL, BENNIE!' he read. 'It certainly was,' he exclaimed, 'And it puts us in the lead. Good thing we've got someone in the team with a bit of go. – Come on now, City; come on, Tolly – make the b-blighters w-work!'

He choked and went off into another coughing fit. By the time he had blown his nose and wiped his eyes, the visiting team had equalized. Mr Bennet couldn't believe it.

'No, it can't be!' he shouted. 'What's the matter with you, ref? – Got your hands over your eyes?'

He went on muttering and scowling at the set. Mrs Mannion came in.

'Good game, is it?' she asked brightly.

'No, it is not, stupid woman,' he growled.

'Oh, dear,' said Mrs Mannion. She sat down in the other armchair. 'Just thought you might like a bit of company,' she said, and glanced at the screen. 'Ooh, look, it says NEVER MIND – what a funny thing for someone to put in with the adverts!'

'Don't be so soft, woman,' snorted Mr Bennet. 'It's not an advert; it's them, isn't it? – It's our two lads up to some trick or other.'

'Do you mean they're putting messages on the television?' said Mrs Mannion. 'Well – I call that really ingenious – fancy, our two boys doing that.'

She smiled proudly at the screen, then

picked up a large paper bag she had
brought with her. She rustled in it for a
moment or two and eventually pulled out
her knitting. She began to knit and the
needles darted to and fro: click, click,
click . . . Mr Bennet lost patience.

'Can't we have a bit of hush, woman?
This is serious – it's not a Women's Bright
Hour, you know – this is football!'

Mrs Mannion folded her knitting on her
lap and sat back to watch. Half-time was
over now. The score was one-all. Tempers
were short. A player from each side was
booked for threatening behaviour. Then
there was a really rough tackle which
brought Tolly down.

'Corner!' yelled Mr Bennet. Mrs
Mannion jumped.

The players took up their positions for
the corner. The ref blew his whistle; Tolly
kicked the ball in. One of the Daffs got his
head to it and cleared the ball up-field. A
City player sent the ball flying back
towards the goal. Tolly gathered himself

and leapt for the ball with his head. He sent
it spinning sideways straight into the top
of the net. The City supporters went wild –
two-one! The TV cameras showed them
swaying to and fro with their scarves above
their heads. The camera cut in to a close-
up of the front rows of the terraces in the
family stand.

'There's Robbie!' cried Mrs Mannion;
Mr Bennet jumped this time.

'Where, woman, where?' he demanded.

'There, look.' She pointed with a knitting
needle. 'Look, there's Robbie, and there's
Steve, and they've changed the message –
GREAT GOAL, BENNIE! it says.'

The last ten minutes of the game dragged
by. The Daffs tried desperately to
equalize, but they were too tired; City
couldn't wait for the final whistle. It went
at last, and there was an outburst of
cheering from the home crowd. The
players looked exhausted; they were ready
for a shower and a rest. They walked
towards the tunnel which led down to the

changing-rooms.

'Quick,' said Robbie, 'the cameras are bound to be focused on the tunnel – hang out the last one.'

Steve jerked the last roll of paper from his jacket. They unrolled it and hung it over the top of the other messages. They stood to attention, each with a hand on one end of the paper. With the other hand they waved at the TV cameras on the platform opposite.

In Mr Bennet's living-room, Mrs Mannion peered at the television screen.

'Well,' she said, 'I can't believe it – it's those boys again. Look, Mr Bennet – oh, and it's a special message for you this time. – Look there.'

Mr Bennet gripped the edge of his knee rug and leaned forward to read.

'HI, BENNIE . . . People keep walking past it,' he grumbled, 'I can't get a good look . . . NAPPY I think it says . . . Nappy? – rubbish, can't be, there're no babies in this house . . .'

He blinked and peered again.

'Oh . . . HAPPY, it says . . . HAPPY BIRT . . . What's a happy birt? . . . Oh, HAPPY BIRTHDAY! . . .'

'Well,' beamed Mrs Mannion. 'There now – what a lovely way to send you greetings, Mr Bennet.'

'Cheeky young devils,' he grumbled, trying not to smile. 'Fancy putting it there for all the world to see . . . But I suppose you have to admit they're an ingenious couple, quite ingenious . . . and it *was* a good City win . . .'

Champion Chang

Chang stood and looked at his mother with anxious eyes.

'You will make sure everything's ready for tomorrow morning at nine o'clock, won't you, Mother?'

'There will be much to do in the morning,' said his mother calmly, 'and you know I always need your help. We shall have the restaurant to clean, the tablecloths to wash and iron, fresh vegetables to fetch from the market – '

'But the match starts at half-past nine. I must be there; I promised Mr Lane. I am one of the best players.'

'One of the best players?' said his mother. 'That is very good, Chang. I will make sure you are ready at nine o'clock.

But now you must help me to switch on this new washing-machine. You understand English, you must help your mother. Look, here is the book the man brought with the machine. It tells you how it works.'

Chang always spoke Chinese at home with his family, but at school he had learnt to speak English like everyone else. His mother said she was too old to learn English now, she would let Chang do that. She had enough to do, working in the family's Chinese restaurant and take-away.

Chang looked at the booklet about the machine and tried to work out what all the knobs and switches were for. His mother had never had an automatic washer before.

'It will be such a help to me,' she said. 'I can put in all the family's washing, all the tablecloths from the restaurant, the towels from the washroom, the aprons from the kitchen – I shan't have to stand over the machine and pull the heavy steaming things into rinsing water and then into my old spin-dryer. Here everything is in one beautiful white machine. While the washer does my washing, I shall be able to cook for the customers.'

Chang's father and big brother came in and they tried to see how it worked, too. But Chang was the only one who could read English, so he kept the booklet in his hand.

'First, load the washer,' he told them.

His mother piled in white tablecloths, overalls and towels.

'And your football clothes,' she said with a smile. 'Then they will be beautiful for tomorrow morning.'

She pushed in his white shorts and red shirt last of all.

' "Close the door," ' read Chang.

She closed the door.

' "Pour in soap powder," ' read Chang.

She poured soap powder into the special drawer at the top.

' "Choose your programme," ' read Chang. ' "A hot wash, a warm wash, a

cool wash or a delicate wash." '

'Oh, a hot wash,' said his mother. 'We
want to get rid of the soya-sauce stains on
the tablecloths.'

' "Push the programme knob," ' read
Chang, "And switch on." '

She did as he said, then everyone stood
back and watched the machine. Suddenly
they heard the sound of water pouring
somewhere inside it. There was a jerk and

a hiccup and – Brrrmmmmm.

'It's working!' they cried.

'Wonderful!' said Chang's mother. 'Now we must get on with our other tasks. We need more rice from the store-room, please, Chang, and then it will be time to open the door for the evening customers.'

When it was his bedtime, Chang went into the kitchen to say goodnight to his mother.

'You won't forget my football clothes, will you?' he reminded her. 'I shall need them at nine o'clock. The match starts at half-past nine. I told Mr Lane I would be there.'

'Don't worry,' she said, stirring the vegetables she was cooking in the wok. 'I shall get up early and take the washing from my wonderful machine. Then I shall iron your football clothes so they will be fresh for you to take to the match.'

She bent and kissed him.

'Goodnight, now, Chang – have a good sleep so you can play well tomorrow.'

Champion Chang

Chang slept very well indeed. The next thing he knew was his mother waking him in the morning. She looked very upset.

'Chang, oh, Chang,' she said. 'My wonderful machine – '

'Has it not worked?' he asked. Perhaps he had not understood the English correctly.

'Oh, yes, it has worked,' she said. 'It has worked too well. Come and see.'

He scrambled out of bed and followed her to the kitchen. The washing basket stood in the middle of the floor full of the clean washing. But Chang stared. His mother wailed: 'Look at it – the colour!'

Only Chang's red football shirt was still the bright colour it had been before. Everything else – the tablecloths, the overalls, the aprons and Chang's shorts – were no longer white, but *pink*, a pale, pale pink.

'Oh, my shirt, my *shorts*!' cried Chang. 'I cannot wear pink shorts. I must wear a red shirt and white shorts, the same as the rest of the team. Oh, oh, what shall I do?'

His mother said: 'I suppose the customers will not mind if our table-cloths are pink – but your shorts must be white, that's true. What can we do?'

They stood there and looked at the pink shorts. Then Chang's mother made up her mind.

'I will go and iron your shirt,' she said. 'You must go to Mrs Wilton's shop and buy some new shorts. Here is a ten-pound note.'

Chang took the note and ran to get dressed. Then he quickly drank a cupful of milk and ran along the street to Mrs Wilton's sports shop. The door was locked. Chang pressed his nose against the glass door. No one was about. He looked impatiently up and down the street. No sign of Mrs Wilton. Then he caught sight of the Post Office clock: quarter to nine. He stood in the shop doorway and jigged up and down.

'Oh, come *on*, Mrs Wilton, come and open your shop soon,' he thought to himself. Then he wondered: 'Suppose she hasn't any white shorts. Or suppose she hasn't my size. Or suppose she's on holiday this week and won't even be opening the shop . . . What shall I do? What shall I tell Mr Lane? Oh, oh . . .'

'Hello, Chang,' said Mrs Wilton. She had suddenly come round the corner. She pulled some keys from her pocket and unlocked the door.

'Waiting for me? My first customer? Come on in.'

Chang followed her into the shop and explained about the washer and the shorts. Mrs Wilton pulled open a few drawers and soon found some dazzling white shorts in Chang's size. She gave him change and stood in the doorway to watch him running back down the street to the Rising Sun, his family's restaurant and take-away.

'Best of luck!' she called.

It was now five-past nine. Chang's mother had a carrier bag ready with his

football socks and boots in and the freshly
ironed shirt laid carefully on top. She
waved goodbye as Chang set off again
towards school.

'May fortune smile on you,' she called
after him.

The rest of the team was already at
school with Mr Lane.

'Ah, Chang,' he said with a smile, 'I
knew you wouldn't let us down. Get
changed and we'll go out on to the field.
The other team will be here any minute.'

Chang changed quickly. He felt very
smart in his freshly ironed shirt and
shining white shorts. He pulled up his red
socks and did up his boots.

'Ready, Chang?' called Mr Lane. Chang
drew a deep breath – what a morning it
had been.

'Yes, I'm ready,' he said.

'Right, then,' said Mr Lane, 'let's go out
there and win.'

And they did, thanks to the only goal of
the match – scored by Chang.

The Lost Tickets

Stewart and his dad hurried home after the match. Their hands were deep in their pockets, as it was a frosty winter's evening, but neither of them noticed the cold. They were going over the game in detail.

'That was awful when Big Jock slipped, wasn't it?' said Stewart. 'Right in the goal mouth – I thought perhaps he'd broken his leg – but then he stretched out and got his toe to the ball – '

'And nudged it over the line,' said his dad.

'He's magic,' said Stewart.

'He never stops, does he?' said Dad. 'And that goal puts them in the Final.'

'Wish we could see it,' said Stewart.

His father pulled the programme out of

his pocket and waved it at Stewart. 'We got another token today. – Just wait till we get home and count up. – I reckon we've got enough to apply for tickets.'

'Dad!' gasped Stewart. 'Tickets for the Final? – Wowee!'

A week after sending off all their programme tokens, back came an envelope containing two green tickets. Stewart hardly dared to take hold of them.

'Gosh,' he whispered, 'tickets for the Final. I've never seen one of these in my life before.'

He examined them again and again until he knew the details by heart. He and his Dad were to be in stand C by 2.30 p.m. on Saturday 6th.

'That's only a week on Saturday,' he kept saying. 'Only nine days to go, and then we'll see Big Jock and the rest of the Rovers in the Final.'

'Only eight days to go,' he said next day, gloating over the tickets again. 'All the lads at school are dead envious – they'd all like to go too.'

'Only seven days to go,' he said next day, 'and then we'll be seeing Big Jock and the team . . .'

His dad looked up from the library book he was reading.

'It says here that he's got one of the best goal averages in first-class football *ever*.'

He looked across at Stewart, who was examining the tickets again.

'You'll wear those tickets out,' he said. 'Put them back in the envelope and let me have them.'

'Oh, Dad,' protested Stewart, 'I won't do them any harm.'

'I don't want to risk losing them,' insisted his dad, holding on to the envelope. 'Now they'll be safe until next Saturday – I'll leave them behind the clock and then we'll know exactly where they are.'

He went back to his football book. Paddi was lying under Dad's chair and looked up pleadingly, so Stewart took her out for a run across the field. Paddi raced ahead and barked at the birds, while Stewart practised kicking at tussocks of grass and dribbling a ball round clumps of thistles.

Next morning everyone was in a rush. Dad was late for work and stood in the kitchen to swallow half a cup of tea.

'I'll be going into town today,' said Mum. 'Anything you want?'

'No, thanks,' said Dad. 'Are you ready,

Stew? – I'll drop you at school. Now where's that file I've got to take? – Down, Paddi, down!'

'Have you finished with your library book?' asked Mum.

'Right – yes, – *down*, Paddi – come on, Stew, let's get going before the traffic builds up. Bye, Sheila.'

That evening Stewart brought Don and Billy home from school with him.

'Go on, Stew,' said Don, 'let's just *look* at them – we won't hurt them.'

'Yes, go on, Stew,' said Billy, 'I've never seen a ticket for the Final.'

'Well, I'm not sure where Dad's put them,' said Stewart. 'He said he'd leave them behind the clock – but they're not here. When he comes in I'll ask him, and you can see them tomorrow.'

Later that evening he said, 'Where've you put the tickets, Dad?'

'Behind the clock,' said his dad absent-mindedly; he was reading the paper.

'No, they're not,' said Stewart.

''Course they are,' said his dad.

'Can't see them,' said Stewart.

His dad crumpled down the newspaper and said in exasperation, ''Course they are.'

He watched Stewart feel behind the clock and look along the mantelpiece. There was no sign of the envelope or the two green tickets. By now Dad was on his feet, also searching frantically.

'I don't believe it,' he said. 'They can't be lost, where are they? – Stewart, have you been messing about and hidden them somewhere?'

'No, of course not,' protested Stewart. 'You had them last. You were sitting there last night, reading that book about Big Jock – '

'That book – ' began Mum.

'My library book,' said Dad, 'where is it?'

'I took it back to the library,' said Mum faintly. 'You said you'd finished with it . . .'

There was a horrified silence.

'I must have used them for a bookmark . . .' whispered Dad.

'Oh, no!' exclaimed Stewart. 'Quick, then – the library's still open – let's get down there!'

Dad drove Stewart at breakneck speed to the library and stopped with a squeal of brakes. They ran up the steps and through the entrance hall. A librarian looked up, surprised, and they breathlessly explained what had happened. He looked horrified too.

'Two tickets for the Final – in a library book?' he exclaimed.

He hurried to the shelf of books on sport; it wasn't there.

'Might be in biography,' he muttered; but it wasn't there either. 'Perhaps someone took it straight out again,' he said, and riffled through the boxes of readers' tickets – but no one seemed to have borrowed it that day.

'Sometimes people put books back on the wrong shelves,' he said helplessly.

'We'll certainly keep a look out for it and
ring you the moment we find it – But of
course there's no guarantee the tickets will
still be in it: it would be very tempting for
someone to keep two tickets for the Final,
especially as Big Jock will be playing . . .'
A gleam came into his eyes. 'I'm a fan of his
myself . . .'

Dad and Stewart drove home in silence at
half the speed, and went indoors.

'No luck?' asked Mum.

They shrugged their shoulders at her and
slumped down on to the settee. Paddi
came out from under Dad's armchair and
wagged her tail as though she wanted to
tell them something.

'No, no walkies for now, Paddi,' said
Stewart, shaking his head. 'We're not in
the mood.'

'I suppose they couldn't have fallen out
of your shopping basket, could they,
Sheila?' asked Dad.

'No, I looked,' said Mum. 'But I did take
the book out of the basket in the market,

34

to make room for the vegetables . . .'

'Oh,' said Dad.

'And I took it out again in the baker's, to put the bread underneath it.'

'Oh!'

'And my basket was so full, that – ' She stopped and bit her lip – 'the book slipped off the top and fell on the ground as I crossed the park on the way to the library . . .'

'Oh, no!' groaned Dad.

'They could be anywhere in town,' said Stewart.

There was a despairing silence.

Paddi crawled out from under Dad's chair and wagged her tail again.

She looked from one despondent face to another, then went back under Dad's chair and came out again – with something between her teeth.

'Hey!' yelled Stewart. Dad jumped. 'Look what Paddi's got!'

'Hey!' yelled Dad. 'It's the envelope!'

Paddi dropped the envelope in front of

them and wagged her tail eagerly; she somehow knew she'd done something clever. Dad hardly dared breathe as he opened the flap of the envelope.

'They're still in there!' he cried.

'Phew – that's a relief,' said Mum. 'They must have slipped down the side of the chair.'

Stewart suddenly felt as though a tight knot in his stomach had untied itself, and he gasped with relief.

'Clever girl, clever Paddi,' he cried. 'Come on, walkies for a clever dog!'

The Final was fantastic. Stewart will never forget it. He and his dad were sitting close enough to get a good view of the Rovers coming up the steps at the end of the match. They were exhausted and sweating, but grinning in triumph, as they received their winners' medals; they had won by three goals to one. The gleaming cup itself was proudly held aloft for all to see by the captain – the one and only Big Jock.

The Canaries' Nests

Mrs Barset was looking forward to Easter, when she would be seventy. Her two grown-up daughters and their husbands and her six grandchildren were all coming out from Norwich to spend the day in the country with her. They were going to bring some extra cups and plates (because she didn't have enough for eleven people), some extra knives and forks, some folding chairs, and all the food for the party. Mrs Barset wasn't going to have to do a thing. She just had to *be* there and enjoy her birthday with the family.

She was hoping the weather would be fine and dry. Then they could carry chairs and everything outside on to her little lawn and have the party in the sunshine. If the

weather was really hot, they could sit under
the apple trees in the tiny orchard next to
the house. Mrs Barset nodded to herself as
she sorted this all out in her mind.

'I think that will work out very well,' she
said, 'and if we drop crumbs, it won't
matter a bit – my birds will soon tidy them
up.'

Mrs Barset was thinking of all the birds
which lived round about. She put out food
and water for them in the winter, and
enjoyed seeing and hearing them in the
spring and summer. She never felt she lived
alone: sparrows nested in the hedges
round her lawn, robins had their home in
the holly bush, and she sometimes caught
sight of a shy brown wren through the ivy
in the hedge-bottom. There were blue-tits,
too, and blackbirds and starlings which
lived in the apple trees, and a speckle-
chested thrush which sang for her every
morning.

So, even though the party was to be for
her and her family, she wanted her friends,

the birds, to be part of it too.

Now there were about three weeks until Easter. Mrs Barset wanted to say thank you to her family for arranging the party. She thought she might give them all a little present – but she only had her pension. That wouldn't be enough to buy ten presents, and she knew her daughters and their husbands wouldn't want her to spend money on them, anyway.

'Perhaps I'll just give the children a little present each,' she thought. 'But what would they like? They get enough sweets as it is. Besides, I'd like to think of something unusual, something they wouldn't expect, something they'd really be pleased to be given.'

Mrs Barset thought and thought.

'What sort of thing are they most interested in?' she wondered. Then she remembered that the two girls and four boys were all football supporters. They all lived in Norwich and supported Norwich Football Club – the team that was called

The Canaries because they wore bright yellow shirts for all their games.

'But how does that help me?' she wondered. Then she recalled seeing some football supporters on television. They had all been wearing woolly hats in their team's colours.

'Of course,' she thought. 'I'll knit each of them a scarf and a woolly hat in the Canaries' colour. I know they'd all like that.'

Next morning she collected her pension from the Post Office and went straight into the village shop, which sold everything. She bought several large balls of soft, bright yellow wool. She hurried home with it and searched out a pair of knitting needles.

'Now to work,' she said. 'I've only got three weeks. I'll have to knit like fury to get six scarves and six woolly hats ready in time for Easter.'

Mrs Barset did work hard. Every spare moment was spent knitting, her needles clicking busily. But she was a good, fast knitter, and one sunny day, not long before Easter, she was ready.

'I'll just put a finishing touch to the hats,' she thought. 'I'll turn them into bobble hats. I'll make a big yellow pom-pom to sew on top of each hat. And as it's such a warm day, I'll sit outside and do it.'

She settled herself in a deck-chair on the lawn. On her lap she had some cardboard, a pair of sharp scissors and all the rest of the yellow wool. She cut two cardboard

circles and began to wind the wood round and round them to make bobbles. When they were finished, they were lovely and fluffy, but rather large and straggly, with loose ends hanging here and there.

'I'd better tidy these up,' thought Mrs Barset. 'They have to be perfectly round when they're finished.'

She began to snip and snip, all round the pom-poms, as she tried to even them up. The little snippets and the long straggly ends fell on the grass. Soon there was quite a pile of pieces of yellow wool on the lawn.

'Oh, bother it,' thought Mrs Barset. 'I know it looks untidy, but it'll have to stay there – I must get these bobbles finished and sewn on to the hats. After that, I'd better get cracking and start to clean the house ready for the party.'

The day arrived at last, bright and warm, just as Mrs Barset had hoped. She went out into the garden and listened to the birds twittering and chirruping. Suddenly, something bright caught her eye. What was

it, up in the apple-tree branches?
Something bright yellow. She walked over
for a closer look. She was amazed when
she saw what it was.

'It's a blackbird's nest,' she said, 'with
bits of my yellow wool woven into it!'

She looked round the garden more
carefully. What was that, deep inside the
holly bush? She went over and peered
between the twigs – the robins had built a
nest, too, with little fringes of bright yellow
wool hanging round it.

'Well I never,' she said, even more
surprised. 'I'll just peep at the wren's nest,'
she thought, and quietly went over to the
ivy in the dark hedge-bottom. There was a
tiny, hidden nest, softly lined with snippets
of fluffy yellow wool.

'Well,' said Mrs Barset, 'that's quite
extraordinary. I've never known anything
like it in my life.'

Then the family arrived, talking and
laughing and wishing Mrs Barset a very
happy birthday. Later on, she gave her

grandchildren the scarves and bobble hats.

'Great,' they said. 'Oh, they're ace, Grandma! Now we can wear them to matches.'

'If you're all very quiet and go on tip-toe,' said Mrs Barset, 'I'll show you some other people who like the Canaries' colour. Come in the garden and take a look. I've got some very unusual Norwich supporters out here – come and see . . .'

The Old Man with the Stick

Earl and James bent over their bikes, which were leaning against the front wall.

'The tyres look OK now,' said Earl. 'I've pumped them as hard as I could.'

'And I've tightened up the screws and cleaned between the spokes,' said James. 'They'll be all right for a while, but they're both old bone-shakers. We're never going to win any races on them.'

'That doesn't worry me, man,' said Earl. 'When I'm grown up, I'm going to earn enough money to save up and buy myself a real racer, the sort they ride in the Milk Race – light-weight frame, narrow tyres, twelve gears, really streamlined. I'll call it "Speedo" or "Gold Streak" or something, and I'll go all over the world riding my bike and winning races and showering the crowd with champagne when I'm world champion.'

'I might just see you around then,' said James, 'when I'm playing professional football. Perhaps I'll be discovered by a talent scout and I'll be taken on by Everton or Spurs or United. Then when I'm really good, they'll let me play for their first team – I might even get to the Cup Final, I might even play at Wembley . . .'

The two boys sat up on the low wall and thought about all the things they hoped to do when they were grown up. It was very hot. James shut his eyes; he could feel the sunshine warming his face. Suddenly he felt Earl nudging him.

'Look, there's that old feller coming,' he said. 'You know, the one with the stick and the little black dog. He lives down near the canal bridge.'

James opened his eyes. The old man was walking slowly along, dragging one leg a little as he walked. He was carrying a string

bag of shopping. A little black dog trotted along just behind him. The boys had often noticed him taking the dog for a walk along the canal bank.

'Perhaps he's limping because he had a car accident,' said Earl.

'Or fell off a ladder or something,' said James.

They watched him for a moment or two.

'Come on, let's go for a ride now,' said Earl. 'We've rested long enough.'

They got on their bikes and set off. First they visited a friend who lived two streets away. Then they went to look at part of a new motorway which was being built through the town. Then they stopped to buy an ice-lolly each and went to sit on a bench while they sucked them.

'Now where?' asked James.

'Down by the canal?' suggested Earl.

They cycled down the road and over the humpy-backed bridge which crossed the canal. Suddenly, a little black dog shot across the road in front of them. Earl slammed on his brakes and wobbled sideways against James. James couldn't keep his balance and fell sideways too. He landed on the road with a crash and a clatter as his bike fell on top of him.

'Ow-oouchh!' he yelled. The old man with the stick came limping out of one of the tiny houses by the canal.

'I'm sorry,' he said. 'So sorry, that was Jet's fault. She ran out of the garden and straight across the road. We've seen you two before, when we've been out for a walk, haven't we? Perhaps she recognized your voices.'

He pulled James's bike upright, then helped James to his feet.

'The wheel has gashed your leg,' said the old man. 'Look, you'd better come into my house and I'll clean you up. You're a bit trembly, it's the shock. Come on, I'll make you a drink. Perhaps your friend can bring the bikes into the garden. – Jet, Jet, come here, naughty girl, come on in!'

The little dog came running back into the garden after her master and the two boys. Earl carefully shut the gate behind him, so she couldn't get out again.

They sat in the old man's little front room. He bathed James's leg and tied a large white handkerchief round the grazed part.

'I haven't got a proper bandage,' he said,
'but this is a very clean hanky. Now I'll
get that tea I promised you.'

He limped to and fro to the kitchen, and
soon the boys were sipping hot tea. James
began to feel better and look around. There
were lots of photographs on the walls –
and most of them seemed to be of football
teams. Many of the players had caps on,
and they were all wearing very long shorts,

almost down to their knees. Some of the photos were a sort of pale brown colour, and showed single players standing with their arms folded, perhaps with one foot resting on a football.

'Did you used to like football?' James asked the old man.

'Like it?' said the old man. 'I loved it. I thought football was the most important thing on earth. I used to play for Manchester City, you know. Look – there's a picture of me at our home ground. We always wore blue and white, you know. There's one of me being presented to the king . . .'

'To the *king*!' said Earl.

'Yes, George the Fifth – that was the queen's grandfather – he came to Wembley to see the Final . . .'

'To Wembley?' echoed James, hardly believing his ears. 'You were in the Cup Final at Wembley?'

'Yes, twice actually,' nodded the old man. 'Look – ' He rummaged in a drawer.

'Here're my two Wembley medals. See, there's the date: 1933 – that was the year we lost. Then we got through to the Final the next year and we won! That was a great day, I can tell you.'

The two boys stared at the old man. He was sitting in his chair smiling at them and stroking Jet's smooth head. He had played for Manchester City nearly sixty years ago. He had played – more than once – in front of a crowd of thousands at Wembley, in front of the king himself! And here they were, sitting in his front room, staring at him, not knowing what to say, suddenly shy.

'I think it's time you both got going,' he said, standing up with the help of his stick. 'Or your families will be wondering where you've got to.'

He went out to the gate with them.

'Tell you what,' he said, as they wheeled their bikes out. 'I've lots of old programmes and cups and medals and such you might like to see. Why don't you drop in again some time? Jet and I like a bit of company, don't we, old girl? Any time.'

James and Earl beamed at one another, then looked back at the old man.

'Great, man,' said Earl.

'Hey, thanks,' said James.

The boys cycled off, waving goodbye. The old man turned back into the house, the little black dog at his side.

'I think they'll be back, Jet,' he said. 'I think they'll be back to see us again quite soon. After all – they've got one of my best white handkerchiefs. They'll have to bring that back, you see. Won't they?'

Late Kick-Off

'Come on, you lot, pile in,' said Mr Russell, holding open the back door of the mini-bus. 'Time's getting on, and we don't want to be late for the first match of the season.'

The members of Greengate School football team scrambled in, clutching their bags of football gear. Mr Russell slammed the door shut and went round to the driving seat. He started the van, switched on the windscreen wipers to clear the drizzle from the windscreen, and turned the van slowly out of the school car-park.

'Pity it's raining,' he said.

'We don't mind a drop of rain,' said a voice from the back. It was Stubby; he had been in the school football team for nearly two years now, and was one of their best players.

'How far is it, sir?' called Gary.

'Oh, we should be at Manor School in about half an hour,' said Mr Russell.

The traffic in town was heavy, so he had to drive slowly. No one said very much. Some of the boys were rather nervous; they'd never played in the school team before.

'I feel sick,' said Stephen.

'Yes, so do I,' whispered Gareth.

Stubby thought he'd better do something to cheer everyone up.

'What do you call a man with a seagull on his head?' he asked brightly.

There was no answer from anyone. The rest of the team stared at him as though he'd grown three ears.

'Come on,' he said, 'it's easy – what do you call a man with a seagull on his head?'

Still no answer.

'Right, Stubby, you'd better tell us,' said Mr Russell from the front. 'What *do* you call a man with a seagull on his head?'

'Cliff,' said Stubby.

There was a short silence. Then the others groaned and laughed and everyone felt better.

'I've heard one of them too,' said John. 'What do you call a woman with a frog on her head?'

No one knew, but Mr Russell was curious.

'What *do* you call a woman with a frog

on her head?' he asked.

'Lily,' said John.

The others giggled. They had left the town behind and were now driving past trees and fields. Alex was sitting just behind Mr Russell and could see the road ahead.

'What's that shining on the road?' he asked.

'Just the rain, I think,' said Mr Russell. Then, as they drove nearer, he suddenly swerved and braked hard. The van jerked to a halt and the boys fell forward against one another.

'Oh, no!' exclaimed Mr Russell. 'I hope that wasn't glass.'

He got out to investigate. The boys crowded to the windows at that side of the van to squint down at him. He was crouching by the offside front wheel. A few moments later he looked in at them with a grim expression on his face.

'I couldn't avoid running over that piece of glass,' he said, 'and it's slit the tyre. The air is escaping fast. We can't go any further in the van or we'll damage the wheel. I can't see any phones or houses on this country road, and it would take me ages to change the wheel. I think I'll have to lock up the van and we'll walk to Manor School and phone the garage from there. – It's only a mile. Put your kagouls on and bring your football gear.'

Everyone groaned and started to pull on anoraks and kagouls.

'What do you call a man with two raincoats?' asked Stubby cheerfully. There was no response from anyone, so he answered himself, 'A man with two raincoats is called Max . . .'

They took no notice of him, but climbed out and started to plod along the side of the road. They kept their heads down, as it was still raining quite hard. There was no sign of any building ahead, only fields and more trees.

'How far is it, sir?' asked Lee.

'Just round that bend in the road – I think,' said Mr Russell.

They plodded on. The only sound was the scrunch of their footsteps and the rain pattering down on their hoods.

'I've thought of another,' said Stubby suddenly. 'What do you call a man who's stolen a telly?'

No one bothered to answer. They were concentrating on walking.

'I'll tell you,' said Stubby. 'A man who's stolen a telly is called Nick.'

There were groans from everyone. Then

silence again. Plod, plod, plod; left foot,
right foot, left foot, right foot; drip, drop,
drip.

'Are we nearly there, sir?' asked Gareth.
'We've gone round that bend now.'

'Ah, well, it must be at the end of these
trees – perhaps,' said Mr Russell. He
didn't sound quite so sure now.

'It's half-past ten already,' said Mark.
'The match was supposed to start ages
ago.'

'They'll wait for us,' said Mr Russell, '– I
hope.'

There were fir trees on both sides of the
road now. The wood seemed very dark,
and as the wind blew, the trees sent down
showers of large drops.

'What do you call a woman on a piece of
bread?' asked Stubby.

'Oh, shut *up*, Stubby!' came several
voices.

'Marj,' said Stubby. 'What do you – '

He broke off gasping as Lee and John
thumped him on the back, and at the same

moment Mr Russell cried, 'There's Manor School, up that drive, look!'

'Hurray,' shouted everyone and started to walk faster and chatter with relief as they turned up the drive. They could see some of the Manor House boys waiting to meet them.

'What do you call a man in a paper bag, sir?' murmured Stubby.

'Russell!' said his teacher. 'And that's to be the last one from you, Stubby. From now on I want you to concentrate on football – just remember what they call my second cousin.'

Stubby stared at him. 'What's that, sir?'

'*Win*,' said Mr Russell.

Something Sporty

Trevor was a bouncy sort of boy, never sitting still for long, always running or jumping or skipping about. He loved playing games, all sorts of games: kicking games, throwing games, batting games, catching games, and he was the fastest runner in the street. He was going to have a birthday soon and he was looking forward to it very much.

'Is there anything you'd specially like for your birthday, Trevor?' asked his mother.

'I haven't really thought about it,' he said, 'but I suppose something to do with games or sport would be nice.'

'Mmm, I'll have to think about it,' said his mum.

Trevor's big sister, Jenny, worked at a

hairdresser's. When she came home at the
end of the week, she had her pay in a pay
packet, and she always gave Trevor fifty
pence to spend. This week she gave him
fifty pence as usual, then she said, 'It's
your birthday soon, isn't it, our kid? Is
there anything you'd specially like?'

'Don't really know,' said Trevor, 'but I
like games and sport. You could look in
the sports shop in town, there might be
something nice in there.'

'Mmm,' said Jenny. 'I'll have to think
about it.'

Next day Trevor's auntie and uncle
phoned up to say they were coming over
at the weekend and they knew it would
soon be Trevor's birthday, so was there
anything special he fancied?

'Well,' said Trevor's mum, 'you know he
always likes to be out playing some game
or other. Perhaps you could get him
something sporty.'

Trevor's best friend, Andrew, was going
to have tea at Trevor's house on his

birthday, so he kept wondering what sort of present he could take round for his friend. He asked his mum what she thought, and they went to the shops together to see if they could get some ideas.

Julie-next-door knew it was nearly Trevor's birthday, too. She was smaller and younger than him, but she wanted to give him a present like everyone else. The trouble was, she didn't get very much pocket-money, so it would have to be a rather *small* present.

At last Trevor's birthday arrived. He was very excited when he woke up and saw a large parcel at the end of his bed. It had a label on it: 'Hope you'll like this. Happy Birthday, from Mum and Dad.'

'Oh, I hope it's something I can play games with,' he thought as he undid the string. You can guess how pleased he was when he found the parcel contained a full-size black-and-white football!

He ran downstairs with it and showed it to Jenny. She was just getting ready to go to work. She was in a rush as usual. She looked in the mirror in the hall, talking to herself: 'Comb, brush, lipstick, purse – oh, bother, I've forgotten something, I'm sure. Now what was it I had to remember this morning?'

She looked at Trevor, pretend-puzzled, then her face brightened: 'Oh, yes, you've got a birthday today, haven't you, our kid?'

She pulled a parcel from under the hall table, smacked a quick, lipsticky kiss on his forehead and said, 'Happy Birthday, Trev. See you, kid.' Then she was away out of the front door and rushing down to the bus stop, late as usual.

Trevor opened the parcel.

'I hope it's something I can play games with,' he thought. Inside the box was a white and orange . . . something, made out of plastic, with a little tube sticking out at the side.

'I think you've got to blow it up,' said his mum, coming downstairs. 'Then when it's blown up as big as it'll go, you push that little plastic stopper thing in the tube. Our Jenny was showing me last night, when you were in bed.'

Trevor blew and blew. The white and orange plastic grew fatter and rounder and bigger. He blew till he was red in the face and looked quite fat and round himself. Quickly he pushed the little white plastic stopper into the tube to stop the air escaping.

'It's a beach-ball,' he said. 'That's great.' He put it next to the black-and-white football on the sideboard. After his breakfast he went out to play. First he played with the beach-ball, throwing it over the clothes-line and running to catch it on the other side before it landed. Then he chalked goal-posts and a net on the brick wall and practised kicking the new football into the centre of the net. Then Andrew came round to play and they thought of even better games with the two of them.

In the afternoon his auntie and uncle

arrived in their car. Trevor and his mum
went out to meet them.

'How's the birthday boy, then?' called
Uncle.

'Give us a kiss, then,' said Auntie.

Trevor stood and let them hug him. Then
he brightened up when his uncle reached
over into the back of the car and brought
out a small square parcel.

'Happy Birthday, Trev,' he said. 'I
thought you might like this, seeing as
you're so keen on sport.'

Inside the box was a bright red cricket
ball, hard and heavy, just like real
cricketers use at real cricket matches.

'Gosh, thanks,' said Trevor. He took it
in the house and put it on the sideboard
next to the football and the beach ball.

Then Andrew came round again. Trevor
hardly recognized him – he was wearing a
white shirt and a tie, and his hair was all
wet and flat on top. Trevor stared.

'Mum said I had to look clean,' said
Andrew with a scowl. 'Here's your

present, Happy Birthday.'

He pushed a large parcel done up in newspaper into Trevor's hands. There were several layers of paper to unwrap.

'It's not a very big present,' explained Andrew, 'so I made the parcel big instead, so you'd have to take longer to unwrap it, then you'd think it was big.'

At last, after Trevor had pulled off about eight layers of paper, he found a tiny rubber ball. It was striped all colours of the rainbow. He bounced it on the floor and it shot high up in the air.

'It's a brill bouncer,' said Trevor. 'Thanks very much.'

He took Andrew inside and showed him the presents on the sideboard: the black-and-white football, the white-and-orange beach ball, the real cricket ball, and now the rainbow bouncy ball.

'See,' he said, 'everyone's given me some sort of ball.'

At that moment there was a scratchy noise at the front door. Trevor knew it

must be Julie-next-door: she always made
that sort of noise because she wasn't tall
enough to reach the doorbell.

'Happy Birthday,' said Julie, handing
him a screwed-up paper bag.

'It's a very little present,' she said, 'but I
only had a penny.'

'Let me guess,' said Trevor, shutting his
eyes and thinking of all the other presents
he'd been given, 'You haven't brought me
some sort of ball, have you?'

'How did you know that?' said Julie, amazed.

Trevor opened the bag and found . . . an aniseed ball.

'Oh, ace,' said Trevor, 'I love these.' He popped it in his mouth. 'You coming in? You can stay for tea if you like; there's beefburgers and banana splits and birthday cake, and then we're going to the park afterwards to play with my other presents – Coming?'

'Yes, great,' said Julie. 'It sounds just the sort of birthday I like.'

Over the Wall

At the bottom of Sammy and Danny's garden was a very high wall. It was so high that they'd never seen over it. But it was a good solid wall for practising goals against. Sammy would get a bit of chalk and draw the goal-posts as high up on the wall as she could reach, then Danny, who was taller, would draw the crossbar along the top. Then they would take it in turns to be goalie and stop the goals, or striker and score as many goals as possible.

One morning they were practising as usual, when Sammy kicked the ball extra hard and extra high.

'Good one,' called Danny, and jumped for it. But the ball flew over her outstretched fingers and disappeared over

the top of the wall. They stood quite still
for a moment or two, staring after the ball.
There was a s-p-l-a-s-h – then silence. The
girls didn't know what to do; the wall was
too high and too smooth to climb.

They mooched back up the garden. Their
father was in the shed doing some
carpentry.

'Hello, you two,' he said, and stopped
hammering.

'Er . . . Dad, do you know what's on the

other side of our big wall?' asked Danny.

'Yes, that's Mr Elliot's garden,' said Dad. 'He lives in that big house round the corner near the bus-stop. I think he's a photographer – Nice chap.'

'Can we just go round and . . . um . . . see if he's in?' asked Sammy.

'I suppose you really mean your football's gone over,' said Dad. 'I knew it would happen one of these days – Go on then – and ask politely.'

Danny and Sammy ran round the corner of the street to the big house. They slowed down as they walked up the long drive.

'Suppose he's cross,' said Sammy.

'Oh, come on,' said her sister, 'it was an accident.'

They knocked at the door, but there was no answer. They knocked again. Still no answer. Then Sammy knocked. The door opened suddenly, and the girls nearly fell in.

'Hello,' said Mr Elliot. 'Sorry, I didn't hear you, I was in my dark room. – What can I do for you?'

'Please can we have our football back?' asked Danny. 'It landed in your splash . . . er, I mean, it splashed on your landing – oh dear . . .'

Both girls burst into giggles. Mr Elliot grinned at them.

'You mean it's landed in my garden pool. You'd better come and help me fish it out.'

They followed him through the house and into the back garden. They soon managed to pull the ball out of the water and dry it on the grass.

'Keen on football, are you?' asked Mr Elliot, looking at them over the top of his glasses. The girls nodded eagerly.

'We're both in the school team,' said Danny.

'Good for you,' he said. 'And good for your school.'

He wrinkled up his face for a moment, thinking, then looked at his watch. 'Look,' he said, 'I'm going to a match this afternoon – to take photographs for the paper. It's only a friendly match, but it will probably be fun. – Like to come?'

Danny and Sammy nodded again, even more eagerly. Mr Elliot walked back home with them and asked their Dad if they could go with him. Dad thought it was a great idea, and said of course they could go.

Soon after lunch Mr Elliot's car drew up at the gate. On the side of the car was written THE EVENING WORLD.

'That's the name of the paper Mr Elliot works for,' said their dad.

They climbed into the car and soon reached the football ground. Mr Elliot parked the car. He went round to the boot and lifted out a heavy black shoulder-bag full of cameras and things he used for photography. Then he took out three flat wooden stools.

'They're for us to sit on,' he explained. 'The grass is always damp, so we photographers sit on these tiny stools. They're not very comfortable, but they're

low down, so we don't spoil anyone's view.
– Here, you two can carry them. And
now, let's pin a label on you both.'

He pulled badges from his pocket and
pinned one on to his lapel. Then he gave
one to each of the girls. Danny read hers
aloud.

'PRESS,' she said.

'Who's going to press us?' asked Sammy.

'It means you're working for the press,'
laughed Mr Elliot. 'That means you're
working for a newspaper. I'm going to be
taking pictures for *The Evening World*,
and you're my helpers – my assistants.
Come on.'

Crowds of people were walking towards
the football ground and queuing up for
tickets, but Mr Elliot led the girls through a
side entrance. They walked round to one
end of the football ground and placed the
little stools near to one of the goal-posts.

'Photographers always sit near the goals,'
said Mr Elliot. 'Because it's the best place
for action shots of the goals being scored. –